A NOTE TO PARENTS

Reading is one of the most important gifts we can give our children. How can you help your child to become interested in reading? By reading aloud!

My First Games Readers make excellent read-alouds and are the very first books your child will be able to read by him/herself. Based on the games children know and love, the goals of these books include helping your child:

- **learn sight words**
- **understand that print corresponds to speech**
- **understand that words are read from left to right and top to bottom**

Here are some tips on how to read together and how to enjoy the fun activities in the back of these books:

Reading Together
- Set aside a special time each day to read to your child. Encourage your child to comment on the story or pictures or predict what might happen next.
- After reading the book, you might wish to start lists of words that begin with a specific letter (such as the first letter of your child's name) or words your child would like to learn.
- Ask your child to read these books on his/her own. Have your child read to you while you are preparing dinner or driving to the grocery store.

Reading Activities
- The activities listed in the back of this book are designed to use and expand what children know through reading and writing. You may choose to do one activity a night, following each reading of the book.
- Keep the activities gamelike and don't forget to praise your child's efforts!

Whatever you do, have fun with this book as you pass along the joy of reading to your child. It's a gift that will last a lifetime!

Wiley Blevins, Reading Specialist
Ed.M. Harvard University

No part of this publication may be reproduced in whole or in part, or stored in a retrieval system, or transmitted in any form or by any means, electronic, mechanical, photocopying, recording, or otherwise, without written permission of the publisher. For information regarding permission, write to Scholastic Inc., Attention: Permissions Department, 555 Broadway, New York, NY 10012.

ISBN 0-439-23562-6

Copyright © 2000 by Hasbro Inc.

CANDY LAND® is a registered trademark of Hasbro Inc.
All rights reserved. Published by Scholastic Inc.

SCHOLASTIC and associated logos are trademarks and/or registered trademarks of Scholastic Inc.

12 11 10 9 8 7 6 5 4 3 2 1   0 1 2 3 4 5 6/0

Illustrated by Joe Kulka
Designed by Peter Koblish

Printed in the U.S.A.
First Scholastic printing, December 2000

CANDY LAND

Have You Seen King Candy?

by Jackie Glassman
Illustrated by Joe Kulka

SCHOLASTIC INC.

New York   Toronto   London   Auckland   Sydney   Mexico City   New Delhi   Hong Kong

Where's King Candy?

Have you seen King Candy?

No. Let us go find him.

Peppermint Park

Have you seen King Candy?

No. Let us go find him.

Have you seen King Candy?

I have not seen King Candy.

Have you seen King Candy?

I have not seen King Candy.

Have you seen King Candy?

I have not seen King Candy.

Have you seen King Candy?

I have not seen King Candy.

Have you seen King Candy?

I have not seen King Candy.

Have you seen King Candy?

You will not find King Candy!

Here he is!

We have found King Candy!

Create a Candy Land Friend

Here are pictures of Candy Land friends from the story. On a separate piece of paper, draw a new Candy Land friend. Give him or her a name.

Do You Know King Candy?

Get together with friends and sing this song to the tune of "Do You Know the Muffin Man?"

First Verse:

Oh, do you know King Candy,
King Candy, King Candy?
Oh, do you know King Candy,
Who lives in Candy Land?

Second Verse:

Oh, yes, I know King Candy,
King Candy, King Candy.
Oh, yes, I know King Candy,
Who lives in Candy Land.

Candy Land Cards

Pretend you are visiting Candy Land. Take a piece of paper and make a postcard to send to your best friend. Here are some examples:

Dear Joe,
Wow! I love Candy Land! Mr. Mint has an awesome swing. See you soon!
Your Pal, Fred

Joe Jones
3 Tree Rd.
Yummyville, NY
93702

Dear Amy,
Candy Land is great. Today I met Princess Lolly. She is so sweet! I miss you. Bye!
Emily

Amy Smith
123 Apple St
Funtown, OH
10358

Count Off!

Who is looking for King Candy in the story? Use the picture clues below to help you remember. Then on a piece of paper, draw all the characters and count how many there are.

C Is For . . .
Which of these yummy snacks begins with the letter *C*?

Inside Candy Castle

What is it like inside Candy Castle? On a piece of paper, draw and write what you imagine.

Candy Land Match

Who lives where? Match each Candy Land friend with his or her home.

Face It!

How do the Candy Land kids feel when they can't find King Candy? Point to the right faces.

How does King Candy feel when his friends find him? Point to the face.

Answers

Count Off!

C Is For . . .
These begin with *C*:

Face It!
This is how the Candy Land kids feel:

This is how King Candy feels:

Candy Land Match